Out in the garden, next to the shed...

under the
clothes line . . .

...in my new bed!

**Magoo! Magoo?
Where are you, Magoo?**

Here in the kitchen, beside the bin . . .

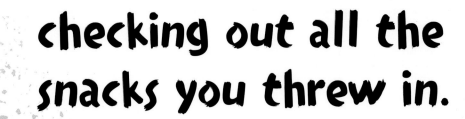

checking out all the snacks you threw in.

Magoo! Magoo?
Where are you,
Magoo?

Just down the hallway,
by this small tree . . .

Magoo!
Magoo?
Where are you,
Magoo?

Out the side gate and off down the street . . .

Magoo!

Magoo?

Where are you,
Magoo?

Here at the playground,
behind the pram . . .

cleaning this baby
covered in jam!

Magoo?

far, **FAR** away from
that mess over there!